"'Father," I said, feeling I might as well get it over while I had him in a good humour, "I had it all arranged to kill my grandmother"'

FRANK O'CONNOR
Born 17 September 1903, Cork City, Ireland
Died 10 March 1966, Dublin, Ireland

'Guests of the Nation' and 'First Confession' were first
published in 1931 and 1951, respectively, in separate
collections of short stories. 'A Story by Maupassant' and
'The Cornet-Player Who Betrayed Ireland' were published
posthumously, in 1969 and 1981, respectively.

ALSO PUBLISHED BY PENGUIN BOOKS
An Only Child and *My Father's Son* · *My Oedipus Complex
and Other Stories*

FRANK O'CONNOR

*The Cornet-Player Who
Betrayed Ireland*

PENGUIN BOOKS

PENGUIN CLASSICS

Published by the Penguin Group
Penguin Books Ltd, 80 Strand, London WC2R ORL, England
Penguin Group (USA) Inc., 375 Hudson Street, New York, New York 10014, USA
Penguin Group (Canada), 90 Eglinton Avenue East, Suite 700, Toronto, Ontario,
Canada M4P 2Y3 (a division of Pearson Penguin Canada Inc.)
Penguin Ireland, 25 St Stephen's Green, Dublin 2, Ireland (a division of Penguin Books Ltd)
Penguin Group (Australia), 250 Camberwell Road, Camberwell, Victoria 3124, Australia
(a division of Pearson Australia Group Pty Ltd)
Penguin Books India Pvt Ltd, 11 Community Centre, Panchsheel Park,
New Delhi – 110 017, India
Penguin Group (NZ), 67 Apollo Drive, Rosedale, North Shore 0632, New Zealand
(a division of Pearson New Zealand Ltd)
Penguin Books (South Africa) (Pty) Ltd, 24 Sturdee Avenue, Rosebank, Johannesburg 2196,
South Africa
Penguin Books Ltd, Registered Offices: 80 Strand, London WC2R ORL, England

www.penguin.com

Selected from *My Oedipus Complex and Other Stories*, first published by Penguin Books 2005
This edition published in Penguin Classics 2011

3

Typeset by Jouve (UK), Milton Keynes
Printed in England by Clays Ltd, St Ives plc

ISBN: 978-0-141-19618-3

www.greenpenguin.co.uk

Contents

The Cornet-Player Who Betrayed Ireland

At this hour of my life I don't profess to remember what we inhabitants of Blarney Lane were patriotic about: all I remember is that we were very patriotic, that our main principles were something called 'Conciliation and Consent', and that our great national leader, William O'Brien, once referred to us as 'The Old Guard'. Myself and other kids of the Old Guard used to parade the street with tin cans and toy trumpets, singing 'We'll hang Johnnie Redmond on a sour apple tree.' (John Redmond, I need hardly say, was the leader of the other side.)

Unfortunately, our neighbourhood was bounded to the south by a long ugly street leading uphill to the cathedral, and the lanes off it were infested with the most wretched specimens of humanity who took the Redmondite side for whatever could be got from it in the way of drink. My personal view at the time was that the

Redmondite faction was maintained by a conspiracy of publicans and brewers. It always saddened me, coming through this street on my way from school, and seeing the poor misguided children, barefoot and in rags, parading with tin cans and toy trumpets and singing 'We'll hang William O'Brien on a sour apple tree.' It left me with very little hope for Ireland.

Of course, my father was a strong supporter of 'Conciliation and Consent'. The parish priest who had come to solicit his vote for Redmond had told him he would go straight to Hell, but my father had replied quite respectfully that if Mr O'Brien was an agent of the devil, as Father Murphy said, he would go gladly.

I admired my father as a rock of principle. As well as being a house-painter (a regrettable trade which left him for six months 'under the ivy', as we called it), he was a musician. He had been a bandsman in the British Army, played the cornet extremely well, and had been a member of the Irishtown Brass and Reed Band from its foundation. At home we had two big pictures of the band after each of its most famous contests, in Belfast and Dublin. It was after the Dublin contest when Irishtown emerged as the premier brass band that there occurred an unrecorded episode in operatic history. In those days the best band in the city was always invited to perform in the Soldiers' Chorus scene in Gounod's

Faust. Of course, they were encored to the echo, and then, ignoring conductor and everything else, they burst into a selection from More's Irish Melodies. I am glad my father didn't live to see the day of pipers' bands. Even fife and drum bands he looked on as primitive.

As he had great hopes of turning me into a musician too he frequently brought me with him to practices and promenades. Irishtown was a very poor quarter of the city, a channel of mean houses between breweries and builders' yards with the terraced hillsides high above it on either side, and nothing but the white Restoration spire of Shandon breaking the skyline. You came to a little footbridge over the narrow stream; on one side of it was a red-brick chapel, and when we arrived there were usually some of the bandsmen sitting on the bridge, spitting back over their shoulders into the stream. The bandroom was over an undertaker's shop at the other side of the street. It was a long, dark, barn-like erection overlooking the bridge and decorated with group photos of the band. At this hour of a Sunday morning it was always full of groans, squeaks and bumps.

Then at last came the moment I loved so much. Out in the sunlight, with the bridge filled with staring pedestrians, the band formed up. Dickie Ryan, the bandmaster's son, and myself took our places at either side of the big drummer, Joe Shinkwin. Joe peered over his big drum

3

to right and left to see if all were in place and ready; he raised his right arm and gave the drum three solemn flakes: then, after the third thump the whole narrow channel of the street filled with a roaring torrent of drums and brass, the mere physical impact of which hit me in the belly. Screaming girls in shawls tore along the pavements calling out to the bandsmen, but nothing shook the soldierly solemnity of the men with their eyes almost crossed on the music before them. I've heard Toscanini conduct Beethoven, but compared with Irishtown playing 'Marching Through Georgia' on a Sunday morning it was only like Mozart in a girls' school. The mean little houses, quivering with the shock, gave it back to us: the terraced hillsides that shut out the sky gave it back to us; the interested faces of passers-by in their Sunday clothes from the pavements were like mirrors reflecting the glory of the music. When the band stopped and again you could hear the gapped sound of feet, and people running and chattering, it was like a parachute jump into commonplace.

Sometimes we boarded the paddle-steamer and set up our music stands in some little field by the sea, which all day echoed of Moore's Melodies, Rossini and Gilbert and Sullivan: sometimes we took a train into the country to play at some sports meeting. Whatever it was, I loved it, though I never got a dinner: I was fed on lemonade, biscuits and sweets, and, as my father spent most of the intervals in the pub, I was sometimes half mad with boredom.

One summer day we were playing at a fête in the grounds of Blarney Castle, and, as usual, the band departed to the pub and Dickie Ryan and myself were left behind, ostensibly to take care of the instruments. A certain hanger-on of the band, one John P., who to my knowledge was never called anything else, was lying on the grass, chewing a straw and shading his eyes from the light with the back of his hand. Dickie and I took a side drum each and began to march about with them. All at once Dickie began to sing to his own accompaniment. 'We'll hang William O'Brien on a sour apple tree.' I was so astonished that I stopped drumming and listened to him. For a moment or two I thought he must be mocking the poor uneducated children of the lanes round Shandon Street. Then I suddenly realized that he meant it. Without hesitation I began to rattle my side drum even louder and shouted 'We'll hang Johnnie Redmond on a sour apple tree.' John P. at once started up and gave me an angry glare. 'Stop that now, little boy!' he said threateningly. It was quite plain that he meant me, not Dickie Ryan.

I was completely flabbergasted. It was bad enough hearing the bandmaster's son singing a traitorous song, but then to be told to shut up by a fellow who wasn't even a bandsman; merely a hanger-on who looked after the music stands and carried the big drum in return for free drinks! I realized that I was among enemies. I quietly put aside the drum and went to find my father. I knew that he could have no idea what was going on behind his back in the band.

I found him at the back of the pub, sitting on a barrel and holding forth to a couple of young bandsmen.

'Now, "Brian Boru's March",' he was saying with one finger raised, 'that's a beautiful march. I heard the Irish Guards do that on Salisbury Plain, and they had the English fellows' eyes popping out. "Paddy," one of them says to me (they all call you Paddy), "wot's the name of the shouting march?" But somehow we don't get the same fire into it at all. Now, listen, and I'll show you how that should go!'

'Dadda,' I said in a whisper, pulling him by the sleeve, 'do you know what Dickie Ryan was singing?'

'Hold on a minute now,' he said, beaming at me affectionately. 'I just want to illustrate a little point.'

'But, dadda,' I went on determinedly, 'he was singing "We'll hang William O'Brien from a sour apple tree."'

'Hah, hah, hah,' laughed my father, and it struck me that he hadn't fully appreciated the implications of what I had said.

'Frank,' he added, 'get a bottle of lemonade for the little fellow.'

'But, dadda,' I said despairingly, 'when I sang "We'll hang Johnnie Redmond", John P. told me to shut up.'

'Now, now,' said my father with sudden testiness, 'that's not a nice song to be singing.'

This was a stunning blow. The anthem of 'Conciliation and Consent' – not a nice song to be singing!

'But, dadda,' I wailed, 'aren't we *for* William O'Brien?'

'Yes, yes, yes,' he replied, as if I were goading him, 'but everyone to his own opinion. Now drink your lemonade and run out and play like a good boy.'

I drank my lemonade all right, but I went out not to play but to brood. There was but one fit place for that. I went to the shell of the castle; climbed the stair to the tower and leaning over the battlements watching the landscape like bunting all round me I thought of the heroes who had stood here, defying the might of England. Everyone to his own opinion! What would they have thought of a statement like that? It was the first time that I realized the awful strain of weakness and the lack of strong principle in my father, and understood that the old bandroom by the bridge was in the heart of enemy country and that all round me were enemies of Ireland like Dickie Ryan and John P.

It wasn't until months after that I realized how many

these were. It was Sunday morning, but when we reached the bandroom there was no one on the bridge. Upstairs the room was almost full. A big man wearing a bowler hat and a flower in his buttonhole was standing before the fireplace. He had a red face with weak, red-rimmed eyes and a dark moustache. My father, who seemed as surprised as I was, slipped quietly into a seat behind the door and lifted me on to his knee.

'Well, boys,' the big man said in a deep husky voice, 'I suppose ye have a good notion what I'm here for. Ye know that next Saturday night Mr Redmond is arriving in the city, and I have the honour of being Chairman of the Reception Committee.'

'Well, Alderman Doyle,' said the bandmaster doubtfully, 'you know the way we feel about Mr Redmond, most of us anyway.'

'I do, Tim, I do,' said the Alderman evenly as it gradually dawned on me that the man I was listening to was the Arch-Traitor, locally known as Scabby Doyle, the builder whose vile orations my father always read aloud to my mother with chagrined comments on Doyle's past history. 'But feeling isn't enough, Tim. Fair Lane Band will be there of course. Watergrasshill will be there. The Butter Exchange will be there. What will the backers of this band, the gentlemen who helped it through so many difficult days, say if we don't put in an appearance?'

'Well, ye see, Alderman,' said Ryan nervously, 'we have our own little difficulties.'

I know that, Tim,' said Doyle. 'We all have our difficulties in troubled times like these, but we have to face them like men in the interests of the country. What difficulties have you?'

'Well, that's hard to describe, Alderman,' said the bandmaster.

'No, Tim,' said my father quietly, raising and putting me down from his knee, ''tis easy enough to describe. I'm the difficulty, and I know it.'

'Now, Mick,' protested the bandmaster, 'there's nothing personal about it. We're all old friends in this band.'

'We are, Tim,' agreed my father. 'And before ever it was heard of, you and me gave this bandroom its first coat of paint. But every man is entitled to his principles, and I don't want to stand in your light.'

'You see how it is, Mr Doyle,' said the bandmaster appealingly. 'We had others in the band that were of Mick Twomey's persuasion, but they left us to join O'Brienite bands. Mick didn't, nor we didn't want him to leave us.'

'Nor don't,' said a mournful voice, and I turned and saw a tall, gaunt, spectacled young man sitting on the window sill. 'I had three men,' said my father earnestly, holding up three fingers in illustration of the fact, 'three men up at the house on different occasions to get me to join other bands. I'm not boasting. Tim Ryan knows who they were.'

'I do, I do,' said the bandmaster.

'And I wouldn't,' said my father passionately. 'I'm not boasting, but you can't deny it: there isn't another band in Ireland to touch ours.'

'Nor a cornet-player in Ireland to touch Mick Twomey,' chimed in the gaunt young man, rising to his feet. 'And I'm not saying that to coddle or cock him up.'

'You're not, you're not,' said the bandmaster. 'No one can deny he's a musician.'

'And listen here to me, boys,' said the gaunt young man, with a wild wave of his arm, 'don't leave us be led astray by anyone. What were we before we had the old band? Nobody. We were no better than the poor devils that sit on that bridge outside all day, spitting into the river. Whatever we do, leave us be all agreed. What backers had we when we started, only what we could collect ourselves outside the chapel gates on Sunday, and hard enough to get permission for that itself? I'm as good a party man as anyone here, but what I say is, music is above politics . . . Alderman Doyle,' he begged, 'tell Mr Redmond whatever he'll do not to break up our little band on us.'

'Jim Ralegh,' said the Alderman, with his red-rimmed eyes growing moist, 'I'd sooner put my hand in the fire than injure this band. I know what ye are, a band of brothers . . . Mick,' he boomed at my father, 'will you desert it in its hour of trial?'

'Ah,' said my father testily, 'is it the way you want me to play against William O'Brien?'

'Play against William O'Brien,' echoed the Alderman. 'No one is asking you to play *against* anyone. As Jim Ralegh here says, music is above politics. What we're asking you to do is to play *for* something: for the band, for the sake of unity. You know what'll happen if the backers withdraw? Can't you pocket your pride and make this sacrifice in the interest of the band?'

My father stood for a few moments, hesitating. I prayed that for once he might see the true light; that he might show this group of misguided men the faith that was in him. Instead he nodded curtly, said 'Very well, I'll play,' and sat down again. The rascally Alderman said a few humbugging words in his praise which didn't take me in. I don't think they even took my father in, for all the way home he never addressed a word to me. I saw then that his conscience was at him. He knew that by supporting the band in the unprincipled step it was taking he was showing himself a traitor to Ireland and our great leader, William O'Brien.

Afterwards, whenever Irishtown played at Redmondite demonstrations, my father accompanied them, but

the moment the speeches began he retreated to the edge
of the crowd, rather like a pious Catholic compelled to
attend a heretical religious service, and stood against
the wall with his hands in his pockets, passing slighting
and witty comments on the speakers to any O'Brienites
he might meet. But he had lost all dignity in my eyes.
Even his gibes at Scabby Doyle seemed to me false, and
I longed to say to him, 'If that's what you believe, why
don't you show it?' Even the seaside lost its attraction
when at any moment the beautiful daughter of a decent
O'Brienite family might point to me and say: 'There is
the son of the cornet-player who betrayed Ireland.'

Then one Sunday we went to play at some idolatrous
function in a seaside town called Bantry. While the meeting was on my father and the rest of the band retired
to the pub and I with them. Even by my presence in
the Square I wasn't prepared to countenance the pro-
ceedings. I was looking idly out of the window when I
suddenly heard a roar of cheering and people began to
scatter in all directions. I was mystified until someone
outside started to shout, 'Come on, boys! The O'Brienites
are trying to break up the meeting.' The bandsmen
rushed for the door. I would have done the same but my
father looked hastily over his shoulder and warned me
to stay where I was. He was talking to a young clarinet-
player of serious appearance.

'Now,' he went on, raising his voice to drown the uproar outside. 'Teddy the Lamb was the finest clarinet-player in the whole British Army.'

There was a fresh storm of cheering, and wild with excitement I saw the patriots begin to drive a deep wedge of whirling sticks through the heart of the enemy, cutting them into two fighting camps.

'Excuse me, Mick,' said the clarinet-player, going white, 'I'll go and see what's up.'

'Now, whatever is up,' my father said appealingly, 'you can't do anything about it.'

'I'm not going to have it said I stopped behind while my friends were fighting for their lives,' said the young fellow hotly.

'There's no one fighting for their lives at all,' said my father irascibly, grabbing him by the arm. 'You have something else to think about. Man alive, you're a musician, not a bloody infantryman.'

'I'd sooner be that than a bloody turncoat, anyway,' said the young fellow, dragging himself off and making for the door.

'Thanks, Phil,' my father called after him in a voice of a man who had to speak before he has collected his wits. 'I well deserved that from you. I well deserved that from all of ye.' He took out his pipe and put it back into his pocket again. Then he joined me at the window and for a few moments he looked unseeingly at the milling crowd outside. 'Come on,' he said shortly.

Though the couples were wrestling in the very gutters no one accosted us on our way up the street; otherwise I feel murder might have been committed. We went to the house of some cousins and had tea, and when we reached the railway station my father led me to a compartment near the engine; not the carriage reserved for the band. Though we had ten minutes to wait it wasn't until just before the whistle went that Tim Ryan, the bandmaster, spotted us through the window.

'Mick!' he shouted in astonishment. 'Where the hell were you? I had men out all over the town looking for you? Is it anything wrong?'

'Nothing, Tim,' replied my father, leaning out of the window to him. 'I wanted to be alone, that's all.'

'But we'll see you at the other end?' bawled Tim as the train began to move.

'I don't know will you,' replied my father grimly. 'I think ye saw too much of me.'

When the band formed up outside the station we stood on the pavement and watched them. He had a tight hold of my hand. First Tim Ryan and then Jim Ralegh came rushing over to him. With an intensity of hatred I watched those enemies of Ireland again bait their traps for my father, but now I knew they would bait them in vain.

'No, no Tim,' said my father, shaking his head, 'I went too far before for the sake of the band, and I paid dear for it. None of my family was ever called a turn-coat before today, Tim.'

'Ah, it is a young fool like that?' bawled Jim Ralegh with tears in his wild eyes. 'What need a man like you care about him?'

'A man have his pride, Jim,' said my father gloomily.

'He have,' cried Ralegh despairingly, 'and a fat lot any of us has to be proud of. The band was all we ever had, and if that goes the whole thing goes. For the love of the Almighty God, Mick Twomey, come back with us to the bandroom anyway.'

'No, no, no,' shouted my father angrily. 'I tell you after today I'm finished with music.'

'Music is finished with us you mean,' bawled Jim. 'The curse of God on the day we ever heard of Red-mond or O'Brien! We were happy men before it . . . All right, lads,' he cried, turning away with a wild and whirl-ing motion of his arm. 'Mick Twomey is done with us. Ye can go on without him.'

And again I heard the three solemn thumps on the big drum, and again the street was flooded with a roaring torrent of music, and though it no longer played for me, my heart rose to it and the tears came from my eyes. Still holding my hand, my father followed on the pavement. They were playing 'Brian Boru's March', his old favourite. We followed them through the ill-lit town and as they turned down the side-street to the bridge, my father stood on the kerb and looked after them as though he wished to impress every detail on his memory. It was only when the music stopped and the silence returned to the narrow channel of the street that we resumed our lonely way homeward.

First Confession

All the trouble began when my grandfather died and my grandmother – my father's mother – came to live with us. Relations in the one house are a strain at the best of times, but, to make matters worse, my grandmother was a real old countrywoman and quite unsuited to the life in town. She had a fat, wrinkled old face, and, to Mother's great indignation, went round the house in bare feet – the boots had her crippled, she said. For dinner she had a jug of porter and a pot of potatoes with – sometimes – a bit of salt fish, and she poured out the potatoes on the table and ate them slowly, with great relish, using her fingers by way of a fork.

Now, girls are supposed to be fastidious, but I was the one who suffered most from this. Nora, my sister, just sucked up to the old woman for the penny she got every Friday out of the old-age pension; a thing I could not do. I was too honest, that was my trouble; and when I was playing with Bill Connell, the sergeant-major's son, and saw my grandmother steering up the path with the jug of porter sticking out from beneath her shawl, I was mortified. I made excuses not to let him come into the house, because I could never be sure what she would be up to when we went in.

When Mother was at work and my grandmother made the dinner I wouldn't touch it. Nora once tried to make me, but I hid under the table from her and took the bread-knife with me for protection. Nora let on to be very indignant (she wasn't, of course, but she knew Mother saw through her, so she sided with Gran) and came after me. I lashed out at her with the bread-knife, and after that she left me alone. I stayed there till Mother came in from work and made my dinner, but when Father came in later Nora said in a shocked voice: 'Oh, Dadda, do you know what Jackie did at dinner-time?' Then, of course, it all came out; Father gave me a flaking; Mother interfered, and for days after that he didn't speak to me and Mother barely spoke to Nora. And all because of that old woman! God knows, I was heart-scalded.

Then, to crown my misfortunes, I had to make my first confession and communion. It was an old woman called Ryan who prepared us for these. She was about the one age with Gran; she was well-to-do, lived in a big house on Montenotte, wore a black cloak and bonnet, and came every day to school at three o'clock when we should have been going home, and talked to us of hell. She may have mentioned the other place as well, but that could only have been by accident, for hell had the first place in her heart.

She lit a candle, took out a new half-crown, and offered it to the first boy who would hold one finger – only one finger! – in the flame for five minutes by the school clock. Being always very ambitious I was tempted to volunteer, but I thought it might look greedy. Then she asked were we afraid of holding one finger – only one finger! – in a little candle flame for five minutes and not afraid of burning all over in roasting hot furnaces for all eternity. 'All eternity! Just think of that! A whole lifetime goes by and it's nothing, not even a drop in the ocean of your sufferings.' The woman was really interesting about hell, but my attention was all fixed on the half-crown. At the end of the lesson she put it back in her purse. It was a great disappointment; a religious woman like that, you wouldn't think she'd bother about a thing like a half-crown.

Another day she said she knew a priest who woke one night to find a fellow he didn't recognize leaning over the end of his bed. The priest was a bit frightened – naturally enough – but he asked the fellow what he wanted, and the fellow said in a deep, husky voice that he wanted to go to confession. The priest said it was an awkward time and wouldn't it do in the morning, but the fellow said that last time he went to confession, there was one sin he kept back, being ashamed to mention it, and now it was always on his mind. Then the priest knew it was a bad case, because the fellow was after making a bad confession and committing a mortal sin. He got up to dress, and just then the cock crew in the yard outside, and – lo and behold! – when the priest looked round there was no sign of the fellow, only a smell of burning timber, and when the priest looked at his bed didn't he see the print of two hands burned in it? That was because the fellow had made a bad confession. This story made a shocking impression on me.

But the worst of all was when she showed us how to examine our conscience. Did we take the name of the Lord, our God, in vain? Did we honour our father and our mother? (I asked her did this include grandmothers and she said it did.) Did we love our neighbours as ourselves? Did we covet our neighbour's goods? (I thought of the way I felt about the penny that Nora got every Friday.) I decided that, between one thing and another, I must have broken the whole ten commandments, all on account of that old woman, and so far as I could see, so long as she remained in the house I had no hope of ever doing anything else.

I was scared to death of confession. The day the whole class went I let on to have a toothache, hoping my absence wouldn't be noticed; but at three o'clock, just as I was feeling safe, along comes a chap with a message from Mrs Ryan that I was to go to confession myself on Saturday and be at the chapel for communion with the rest. To make it worse, Mother couldn't come with me and sent Nora instead.

Now, that girl had ways of tormenting me that Mother never knew of. She held my hand as we went down the hill, smiling sadly and saying how sorry she was for me, as if she were bringing me to the hospital for an operation.

'Oh, God help us!' she moaned. 'Isn't it a terrible pity you weren't a good boy? Oh, Jackie, my heart bleeds for you! How will you ever think of all your sins? Don't forget you have to tell him about the time you kicked Gran on the shin.'

'Lemme go!' I said, trying to drag myself free of her. 'I don't want to go to confession at all.'

'But sure, you'll have to go to confession, Jackie,' she replied in the same regretful tone. 'Sure, if you didn't, the parish priest would be up to the house, looking for you. 'Tisn't, God knows, that I'm not sorry for you. Do you remember the time you tried to kill me with the bread-knife under the table? And the language you used

21

to me? I don't know what he'll do with you at all, Jackie. He might have to send you up to the bishop.'

I remember thinking bitterly that she didn't know the half of what I had to tell – if I told it. I knew I couldn't tell it, and understood perfectly why the fellow in Mrs Ryan's story made a bad confession; it seemed to me a great shame that people wouldn't stop criticizing him. I remember that steep hill down to the church, and the sunlit hillsides beyond the valley of the river, which I saw in the gaps between the houses like Adam's last glimpse of Paradise.

Then, when she had manoeuvred me down the long flight of steps to the chapel yard, Nora suddenly changed her tone. She became the raging malicious devil she really was.

'There you are!' she said with a yelp of triumph, hurling me through the church door. 'And I hope he'll give you the penitential psalms, you dirty little caffler.'

I knew then I was lost, given up to eternal justice. The door with the coloured-glass panels swung shut behind me, the sunlight went out and gave place to deep shadow, and the wind whistled outside so that the silence within seemed to crackle like ice under my feet. Nora sat in front of me by the confession box. There were a couple of old women ahead of her, and then a miserable-looking poor devil came and wedged me in at the other side, so that I couldn't escape even if I had the courage. He joined his hands and rolled his eyes in the direction of the roof, muttering aspirations in an anguished tone, and I wondered had he a grandmother too. Only a grandmother could account for a fellow behaving in that heart-broken way, but he was better off than I, for he at least could go and confess his sins; while I would make a bad confession and then die in the night and be continually coming back and burning people's furniture.

Nora's turn came, and I heard the sound of something slamming, and then her voice as if butter wouldn't melt in her mouth, and then another slam, and out she came. God, the hypocrisy of women! Her eyes were lowered, her head was bowed, and her hands were joined very low down on her stomach, and she walked up the aisle to the side altar looking like a saint. You never saw such an exhibition of devotion; and I remembered the devilish malice with which she had tormented me all the way from our door, and wondered were all religious people like that, really. It was my turn now. With the fear of damnation in my soul I went in, and the confessional door closed of itself behind me.

It was pitch-dark and I couldn't see priest or anything else. Then I really began to be frightened. In the darkness it was a matter between God and me, and He had all the odds. He knew what my intentions were before

I even started; I had no chance. All I had ever been told about confession got mixed up in my mind, and I knelt to one wall and said: 'Bless me, father, for I have sinned; this is my first confession.' I waited for a few minutes, but nothing happened, so I tried it on the other wall. Nothing happened there either. He had me spotted all right.

It must have been then that I noticed the shelf at about one height with my head. It was really a place for grown-up people to rest their elbows, but in my distracted state I thought it was probably the place you were supposed to kneel. Of course, it was on the high side and not very deep, but I was always good at climbing and managed to get up all right. Staying up was the trouble. There was room only for my knees, and nothing you could get a grip on but a sort of wooden moulding a bit above it. I held on to the moulding and repeated the words a little louder, and this time something happened all right. A slide was slammed back; a little light entered the box, and a man's voice said: 'Who's there?'

''Tis me, father,' I said for fear he mightn't see me and go away again. I couldn't see him at all. The place the voice came from was under the moulding, about level with my knees, so I took a good grip of the moulding and swung myself down till I saw the astonished face of a young priest looking up at me. He had to put his head on one side to see me, and I had to put mine on one side to see him, so we were more or less talking to one another upside-down. It struck me as a queer way of hearing confessions, but I didn't feel it my place to criticize.

'Bless me, father, for I have sinned; this is my first confession,' I rattled off all in one breath, and swung myself down the least shade more to make it easier for him.

'What are you doing up there?' he shouted in an angry voice; and the strain the politeness was putting on my hold of the moulding, and the shock of being addressed in such an uncivil tone, were too much for me. I lost my grip, tumbled, and hit the door an unmerciful wallop before I found myself flat on my back in the middle of the aisle. The people who had been waiting stood up with their mouths open. The priest opened the door of the middle box and came out, pushing his biretta back from his forehead; he looked something terrible. Then Nora came scampering down the aisle.

'Oh, you dirty little caffler!' she said. 'I might have known you'd do it. I might have known you'd disgrace me. I can't leave you out of my sight for one minute.'

Before I could even get to my feet to defend myself she bent down and gave me a clip across the ear. This reminded me that I was so stunned I had even forgotten to cry, so that people might think I wasn't hurt at all, when in fact I was probably maimed for life. I gave a roar out of me.

'What's all this about?' the priest hissed, getting angrier than ever and pushing Nora off me. 'How dare you hit the child like that, you little vixen?'

'But I can't do my penance with him, father,' Nora cried, cocking an outraged eye up at him.

'Well, go and do it, or I'll give you some more to do,' he said, giving me a hand up. 'Was it coming to confession you were, my poor man?' he asked me.

''Twas, father,' said I with a sob.

'Oh,' he said respectfully, 'a big hefty fellow like you must have terrible sins. Is this your first?'

''Tis, father,' said I.

'Worse and worse,' he said gloomily. 'The crimes of a lifetime. I don't know will I get rid of you at all today. You'd better wait now till I'm finished with these old ones. You can see by the looks of them they haven't much to tell.'

'I will, father,' I said with something approaching joy.

The relief of it was really enormous. Nora stuck out her tongue at me from behind his back, but I couldn't even be bothered retorting. I knew from the very moment that man opened his mouth that he was intelligent above the ordinary. When I had time to think, I saw how right I was. It only stood to reason that a fellow confessing after seven years would have more to tell than people that went every week. The crimes of a lifetime, exactly as he said. It was only what he expected, and the rest was the cackle of old women and girls with their talk of hell, the bishop, and the penitential psalms. That was all they knew. I started to make my examination of conscience, and barring the one bad business of my grandmother it didn't seem so bad.

The next time, the priest steered me into the confession box himself and left the shutter back the way I could see him get in and sit down at the further side of the grille from me.

'Well, now,' he said, 'what do they call you?'

'Jackie, father,' said I.

'And what's a-trouble to you, Jackie?'

'Father,' I said, feeling I might as well get it over while I had him in good humour, 'I had it all arranged to kill my grandmother.'

He seemed a bit shaken by that, all right, because he said nothing for quite a while.

'My goodness,' he said at last, 'that'd be a shocking thing to do. What put that into your head?'

'Father,' I said, feeling very sorry for myself, 'she's an awful woman.'

'Is she?' he asked. 'What way is she awful?'

'She takes porter, father,' I said, knowing well from

the way Mother talked of it that this was a mortal sin, and hoping it would make the priest take a more favourable view of my case.

'Oh, my!' he said, and I could see he was impressed.

'And snuff, father,' said I.

'That's a bad case, sure enough, Jackie,' he said.

'And she goes round in her bare feet, father,' I went on in a rush of self-pity, 'and she know I don't like her, and she gives pennies to Nora and none to me, and my da sides with her and flakes me, and one night I was so heart-scalded I made up my mind I'd have to kill her.'

'And what would you do with the body?' he asked with great interest.

'I was thinking I could chop that up and carry it away in a barrow I have,' I said.

'Begor, Jackie,' he said, 'do you know you're a terrible child?'

'I know, father,' I said, for I was just thinking the same thing myself. 'I tried to kill Nora too with a bread-knife under the table, only I missed her.'

'Is that the little girl that was beating you just now?' he asked.

''Tis, father.'

'Someone will go for her with a bread-knife one day, and he won't miss her,' he said rather cryptically. 'You must have great courage. Between ourselves, there's a lot of people I'd like to do the same to but I'd never have the nerve. Hanging is an awful death.'

'Is it, father?' I asked with the deepest interest – I was always very keen on hanging. 'Did you ever see a fellow hanged?'

'Dozens of them,' he said solemnly. 'And they all died roaring.'

'Jay!' I said.

'Oh, a horrible death!' he said with great satisfaction. 'Lots of the fellows I saw killed their grandmothers too, but they all said 'twas never worth it.'

He had me there for a full ten minutes talking, and then walked out the chapel yard with me. I was genuinely sorry to part with him, because he was the most entertaining character I'd ever met in the religious line. Outside, after the shadow of the church, the sunlight was like the roaring of waves on a beach; it dazzled me; and when the frozen silence melted and I heard the screech of trams on the road my heart soared. I knew now I wouldn't die in the night and come back, leaving marks on my mother's furniture. It would be a great worry to her, and the poor soul had enough.

Nora was sitting on the railing, waiting for me, and she put on a very sour puss when she saw the priest with me. She was mad jealous because a priest had never come out of the church with her.

'Well,' she asked coldly, after he left me, 'what did he give you?'

'Three Hail Marys,' I said.

'Three Hail Marys,' she repeated incredulously. 'You mustn't have told him anything.'

'I told him everything,' I said confidently.

'About Gran and all?'

'About Gran and all.'

(All she wanted was to be able to go home and say I'd made a bad confession.)

'Did you tell him you went for me with the bread-knife?' she asked with a frown.

'I did to be sure.'

'And he only gave you three Hail Marys?'

'That's all.'

She slowly got down from the railing with a baffled air. Clearly, this was beyond her. As we mounted the steps back to the main road she looked at me suspiciously.

'What are you sucking?' she asked.

'Bullseyes.'

'Was it the priest gave them to you?'

''Twas.'

'Lord God,' she wailed bitterly, 'some people have all the luck! 'Tis no advantage to anybody trying to be good. I might just as well be a sinner like you.'

Guests of the Nation

At dusk the big Englishman, Belcher, would shift his long legs out of the ashes and say, 'Well, chums, what about it?' and Noble or myself would say, 'All right, chum' (for we had picked up some of their curious expressions), and the little Englishman, Hawkins, would light the lamp and bring out the cards. Sometimes Jeremiah Donovan would come up and supervise the game, and get excited over Hawkins's cards, which he always played badly, and shout at him as if he was one of our own, 'Ah, you divil, why didn't you play the tray?'

But ordinarily Jeremiah was a sober and contented poor devil like the big Englishman, Belcher, and was looked up to only because he was a fair hand at documents, though he was slow even with them. He wore a small cloth hat and big gaiters over his long pants, and you seldom saw him with his hands out of his pockets. He reddened when you talked to him, tilting from toe to heel and back, and looking down all the time at his big farmer's feet. Noble and myself used to make fun of his broad accent, because we were both from the town.

I could not at the time see the point of myself and Noble guarding Belcher and Hawkins at all, for it was my belief that you could have planted that pair down anywhere from this to Claregalway and they'd have taken root there like a native weed. I never in my short experience saw two men take to the country as they did.

They were passed on to us by the Second Battalion when the search for them became too hot, and Noble and myself, being young, took them over with a natural feeling of responsibility, but Hawkins made us look like fools when he showed that he knew the country better than we did.

'You're the bloke they call Bonaparte,' he says to me. 'Mary Brigid O'Connell told me to ask what you'd done with the pair of her brother's socks you borrowed.'

For it seemed, as they explained it, that the Second had little evenings, and some of the girls of the neighbourhood turned up, and, seeing they were such decent chaps, our fellows could not leave the two Englishmen out. Hawkins learned to dance 'The Walls of Limerick', 'The Siege of Ennis' and 'The Waves of Tory' as well as any of them, though he could not return the compliment, because our lads at that time did not dance foreign dances on principle.

So whatever privileges Belcher and Hawkins had with the Second they just took naturally with us, and after the first couple of days we gave up all pretence of keeping an eye on them. Not that they could have got far, because they had accents you could cut with a knife, and wore khaki tunics and overcoats with civilian pants and boots, but I believe myself they never had any idea of escaping and were quite content to be where they were.

It was a treat to see how Belcher got off with the old woman in the house where we were staying. She was a great warrant to scold, and cranky even with us, but before ever she had a chance of giving our guests, as I may call them, a lick of her tongue, Belcher had made her his friend for life. She was breaking sticks, and Belcher, who had not been more than ten minutes in the house, jumped up and went over to her.

'Allow me, madam,' he said, smiling his queer little smile. 'Please allow me,' and he took the hatchet from her. She was too surprised to speak, and after that, Belcher would be at her heels, carrying a bucket, a basket or a load of turf. As Noble said, he got into looking before she leapt, and hot water, or any little thing she wanted, Belcher would have ready for her. For such a huge man (and though I am five foot ten myself I had to look up at him) he had an uncommon lack of speech. It took us a little while to get used to him, walking in and out like a ghost, without speaking. Especially because Hawkins talked enough for a platoon it was strange to hear Belcher with his toes in the ashes come out with a solitary 'Excuse me, chum,' or 'That's right, chum.' His one and only passion was cards, and he was a remarkably good card player. He could have skinned myself and Noble, but whatever we lost to him, Hawkins lost to us, and Hawkins only played with the money Belcher gave him.

Hawkins lost to us because he had too much old gab, and we probably lost to Belcher for the same reason. Hawkins and Noble argued about religion into the early hours of the morning, and Hawkins worried the life out of Noble, who had a brother a priest, with a string of questions that would puzzle a cardinal. Even in treating of holy subjects, Hawkins had a deplorable tongue. I never met a man who could mix such a variety of cursing and bad language into any argument. He was a terrible man, and a fright to argue. He never did a stroke of work, and when he had no one else to argue with, he got stuck in the old woman.

He met his match in her, for when he tried to get her

to complain profanely of the drought she gave him a great come-down by blaming it entirely on Jupiter Pluvius (a deity neither Hawkins nor I had ever heard of, though Noble said that among the pagans it was believed that he had something to do with the rain). Another day he was swearing at the capitalists for starting the German war when the old lady laid down her iron, puckered up her little crab's mouth and said: 'Mr Hawkins, you can say what you like about the war, and think you'll deceive me because I'm only a simple poor country-woman, but I know what started the war. It was the Italian Count that stole the heathen divinity out of the temple in Japan. Believe me, Mr Hawkins, nothing but sorrow and want can follow people who disturb the hidden powers.'

A queer old girl, all right.

One evening we had our tea and Hawkins lit the lamp and we all sat into cards. Jeremiah Donovan came in too, and sat and watched us for a while, and it suddenly struck me that he had no great love for the two Englishmen. It came as a surprise to me because I had noticed nothing of it before.

Late in the evening a really terrible argument blew up between Hawkins and Noble about capitalists and priests and love of country.

'The capitalists pay the priests to tell you about the next world so that you won't notice what the bastards are up to in this,' said Hawkins.

'Nonsense, man!' said Noble, losing his temper. 'Before ever a capitalist was thought of people believed in the next world.'

Hawkins stood up as though he was preaching.

'Oh, they did, did they?' he said with a sneer. 'They believed all the things you believe – isn't that what you mean? And you believe God created Adam, and Adam created Shem, and Shem created Jehoshaphat. You believe all that silly old fairy-tale about Eve and Eden and the apple. Well listen to me, chum! If you're entitled to a silly belief like that, I'm entitled to my own silly belief – which is that the first thing your God created was a bleeding capitalist, with morality and Rolls-Royce complete. Am I right, chum?' he says to Belcher.

'You're right, chum,' says Belcher with a smile, and he got up from the table to stretch his long legs into the fire and stroke his moustache. So, seeing that Jeremiah Donovan was going, and that there was no knowing when the argument about religion would be over, I went out with him. We strolled down to the village together, and then he stopped, blushing and mumbling, and said I should be behind, keeping guard. I didn't like the tone he took with me, and anyway I was bored with life in the cottage, so I replied by asking what the hell we wanted to guard them for at all.

He looked at me in surprise and said: 'I thought you knew we were keeping them as hostages.'

'Hostages?' I said.

'The enemy have prisoners belonging to us, and now they're talking of shooting them,' he said. 'If they shoot our prisoners, we'll shoot theirs.'

'Shoot Belcher and Hawkins?' I said.

'What else did you think we were keeping them for?' he said.

'Wasn't it very unforeseen of you not to warn Noble and myself of that in the beginning?' I said.

'How was it?' he said. 'You might have known that much.'

'We could not know it, Jeremiah Donovan,' I said. 'How could we when they were on our hands so long?'

'The enemy have our prisoners as long and longer,' he said.

'That's not the same thing at all,' said I.

'What difference is there?' said he.

I couldn't tell him, because I knew he wouldn't understand. If it was only an old dog that you had to take to the vet's, you'd try and not get too fond of him, but Jeremiah Donovan was not a man who would ever be in danger of that.

'And when is this to be decided?' I said.

'We might hear tonight,' he said. 'Or tomorrow or the next day at latest. So if it's only hanging round that's a trouble to you, you'll be free soon enough.'

It was not the hanging round that was a trouble to me at all by this time. I had worse things to worry about. When I got back to the cottage the argument was still on. Hawkins was holding forth in his best style, maintaining that there was no next world, and Noble saying that there was; but I could see that Hawkins had had the best of it.

'Do you know what, chum?' he was saying with a saucy smile. 'I think you're just as big a bleeding unbeliever as I am. You say you believe in the next world, and you know just as much about the next world as I do, which is sweet damn-all. What's heaven? You don't know. Where's heaven? You don't know. You know sweet damn-all! I ask you again, do they wear wings?'

'Very well, then,' said Noble. 'They do. Is that enough for you? They do wear wings.'

'Where do they get them then? Who makes them? Have they a factory for wings? Have they a sort of store where you hand in your chit and take your bleeding wings?'

'You're an impossible man to argue with,' said Noble. 'Now, listen to me –' And they were off again.

It was long after midnight when we locked up and

went to bed. As I blew out the candle I told Noble. He took it very quietly. When we'd been in bed about an hour he asked if I thought we should tell the Englishmen. I didn't, because I doubted if the English would shoot our men. Even if they did, the Brigade officers, who were always up and down to the Second Battalion and knew the Englishmen well, would hardly want to see them plugged. 'I think so too,' said Noble. 'It would be great cruelty to put the wind up them now.'

'It was very unforeseen of Jeremiah Donovan, anyhow,' said I.

It was next morning that we found it so hard to face Belcher and Hawkins. We went about the house all day, scarcely saying a word. Belcher didn't seem to notice; he was stretched into the ashes as usual, with his usual look of waiting in quietness for something unforeseen to happen, but Hawkins noticed it and put it down to Noble's being beaten in the argument of the night before.

'Why can't you take the discussion in the proper spirit?' he said severely. 'You and your Adam and Eve! I'm a Communist, that's what I am. Communist or Anarchist, it all comes to much the same thing.' And he went round the house, muttering when the fit took him: 'Adam and Eve! Adam and Eve! Nothing better to do with their time than pick bleeding apples!'

*

I don't know how we got through that day, but I was very glad when it was over, the tea things were cleared away, and Belcher said in his peaceable way: 'Well, chums, what about it?' We sat round the table and Hawkins took out the cards, and just then I heard Jeremiah Donovan's footsteps on the path and a dark presentiment crossed my mind. I rose from the table and caught him before he reached the door.

'What do you want?' I asked.

'I want those two soldier friends of yours,' he said, getting red.

'Is that the way, Jeremiah Donovan?' I asked.

'That's the way. There were four of our lads shot this morning, one of them a boy of sixteen.'

'That's bad,' I said.

At that moment Noble followed me out, and the three of us walked down the path together, talking in whispers. Feeney, the local intelligence officer, was standing by the gate.

'What are you going to do about it?' I asked Jeremiah Donovan.

'I want you and Noble to get them out; tell them they're being shifted again; that'll be the quietest way.'

'Leave me out of that,' said Noble under his breath.

Jeremiah Donovan looked at him hard.

'All right,' he says. 'You and Feeney get a few tools

from the shed and dig a hole by the far end of the bog. Bonaparte and myself will be after you. Don't let anyone see you with the tools. I wouldn't like it to go beyond ourselves.'

We saw Feeney and Noble go round to the shed and went in ourselves. I left Jeremiah Donovan to do the explanations. He told them that he had orders to send them back to the Second Battalion. Hawkins let out a mouthful of curses, and you could see that though Belcher didn't say anything, he was a bit upset too. The old woman was for having them stay in spite of us, and she didn't stop advising them until Jeremiah Donovan lost his temper and turned on her. He had a nasty temper, I noticed. It was pitch-dark in the cottage by this time, but no one thought of lighting the lamp, and in the darkness the two Englishmen fetched their topcoats and said good-bye to the old woman.

'Just as a man makes a home of a bleeding place, some bastard at headquarters thinks you're too cushy and shunts you off,' said Hawkins, shaking her hand.

'A thousand thanks, madam,' said Belcher. 'A thousand thanks for everything' – as though he'd made it up.

We went round to the back of the house and down towards the bog. It was only then that Jeremiah Donovan told them. He was shaking with excitement.

'There were four of our fellows shot in Cork this morning and now you're to be shot as a reprisal.'

'What are you talking about?' snaps Hawkins. 'It's bad enough being mucked about as we are without having to put up with your funny jokes.'

'It isn't a joke,' says Donovan. 'I'm sorry, Hawkins, but it's true,' and begins on the usual rigmarole about duty and how unpleasant it is. I never noticed that people who talk a lot about duty find it much of a trouble to them.

'Oh, cut it out!' said Hawkins.

'Ask Bonaparte,' said Donovan, seeing that Hawkins wasn't taking him seriously. 'Isn't it true, Bonaparte?'

'It is,' I said, and Hawkins stopped.

'Ah, for Christ's sake, chum!'

'I mean it, chum,' I said.

'You don't sound as if you meant it.'

'If he doesn't mean it, I do,' said Donovan, working himself up.

'What have you against me, Jeremiah Donovan?'

'I never said I had anything against you. But why did your people take out four of your prisoners and shoot them in cold blood?'

He took Hawkins by the arm and dragged him on, but it was impossible to make him understand that we were in earnest. I had the Smith and Wesson in my pocket and I kept fingering it and wondering what I'd do if they put up a fight for it or ran, and wishing to

God they'd do one or the other. I knew if they did run for it, that I'd never fire on them. Hawkins wanted to know was Noble in it, and when we said yes, he asked us why Noble wanted to plug him. Why did any of us want to plug him? What had he done to us? Weren't we all chums? Didn't we understand him and didn't he understand us? Did we imagine for an instant that he'd shoot us for all the so-and-so officers in the so-and-so British Army?

By this time we'd reached the bog, and I was so sick I couldn't even answer him. We walked along the edge of it in the darkness, and every now and then Hawkins would call a halt and begin all over again, as if he was wound up, about our being chums, and I knew that nothing but the sight of the grave would convince him that we had to do it. And all the time I was hoping that something would happen; that they'd run for it or that Noble would take over the responsibility from me. I had the feeling that it was worse on Noble than on me.

At last we saw the lantern in the distance and made towards it. Noble was carrying it, and Feeney was standing somewhere in the darkness behind him, and the picture of them so still and silent in the bogland brought it home to me that we were in earnest, and banished the last bit of hope I had.

Belcher, on recognizing Noble, said: 'Hallo, chum,' in his quiet way, but Hawkins flew at him at once, and the argument began all over again, only this time Noble had nothing to say for himself and stood with his head down, holding the lantern between his legs.

It was Jeremiah Donovan who did the answering. For the twentieth time, as though it was haunting his mind, Hawkins asked if anybody thought he'd shoot Noble.

'Yes, you would,' said Jeremiah Donovan.

'No, I wouldn't, damn you!'

'You would, because you'd know you'd be shot for not doing it.'

'I wouldn't, not if I was to be shot twenty times over. I wouldn't shoot a pal. And Belcher wouldn't – isn't that right, Belcher?'

'That's right chum,' Belcher said, but more by way of answering the question than of joining in the argument. Belcher sounded as though whatever unforeseen thing he'd always been waiting for had come at last.

'Anyway, who says Noble would be shot if I wasn't? What do you think I'd do if I was in his place, out in the middle of a blasted bog?'

'What would you do?' asked Donovan.

'I'd go with him wherever he was going, of course. Share my last bob with him and stick by him through thick and thin. No one can ever say of me that I let down a pal.'

'We had enough of this,' said Jeremiah Donovan, cocking his revolver. 'Is there any message you want to send?'

'No, there isn't.'

'Do you want to say your prayers?'

Hawkins came out with a cold-blooded remark that even shocked me and turned on Noble again.

'Listen to me, Noble,' he said. 'You and me are chums. You can't come over to my side, so I'll come over to your side. That show you I mean what I say? Give me a rifle and I'll go along with you and the other lads.'

Nobody answered him. We knew that was no way out.

'Hear what I'm saying?' he said. 'I'm through with it. I'm a deserter or anything else you like. I don't believe in your stuff but it's no worse than mine. That satisfy you?'

Noble raised his head, but Donovan began to speak and he lowered it again without replying.

'For the last time, have you any messages to send?' said Donovan in a cold, excited sort of voice.

'Shut up, Donovan! You don't understand me, but these lads do. They're not the sort to make a pal and kill a pal. They're not the tools of any capitalist.'

I alone of the crowd saw Donovan raise his Webley to the back of Hawkins's neck, and as he did so I shut my eyes and tried to pray. Hawkins had begun to say something else when Donovan fired, and as I opened my eyes at the bang, I saw Hawkins stagger at the knees and lie out flat at Noble's feet, slowly and as quiet as a kid falling asleep, with the lantern-light on his lean legs and bright farmer's boots. We all stood very still, watching him settle out in the last agony.

Then Belcher took out a handkerchief and began to tie it about his own eyes (in our excitement we'd forgotten to do the same for Hawkins), and, seeing it wasn't big enough, turned and asked for the loan of mine. I gave it to him and he knotted the two together and pointed with his foot at Hawkins.

'He's not quite dead,' he said. 'Better give him another.'

Sure enough, Hawkins's left knee was beginning to rise. I bent down and put my gun to his head; then, recollecting myself, I got up again. Belcher understood what was in my mind.

'Give him his first,' he said. 'I don't mind. Poor bastard, we don't know what's happening to him now.'

I knelt and fired. By this time I didn't seem to know what I was doing. Belcher, who was fumbling a bit awkwardly with the handkerchiefs, came out with a laugh as he heard the shot. It was the first time I had heard him laugh and it sent a shudder down my back; it sounded so unnatural.

'Poor bugger!' he said quietly. 'And last night he was so curious about it all. It's very queer, chums, I always think. Now he knows as much about it as they'll ever let him know, and last night he was all in the dark.'

Donovan helped him to tie the handkerchiefs about his eyes. 'Thanks, chum,' he said. Donovan asked if there were any messages he wanted sent.

'No, chum,' he said. 'Not for me. If any of you would like to write to Hawkins's mother, you'll find a letter from her in his pocket. He and his mother were great chums. But my missus left me eight years ago. Went away with another fellow and took the kid with her. I like the feeling of a home, as you may have noticed, but I couldn't start another again after that.'

It was an extraordinary thing, but in those few minutes Belcher said more than in all the weeks before. It was just as if the sound of the shot had started a flood of talk in him and he could go on the whole night like that, quite happily, talking about himself. We stood around like fools now that he couldn't see us any longer. Donovan looked at Noble, and Noble shook his head. Then Donovan raised his Webley, and at that moment Belcher gave his queer laugh again. He may have thought

we were talking about him, or perhaps he noticed the
same thing I'd noticed and couldn't understand it.

'Excuse me, chums,' he said. 'I feel I'm talking the
hell of a lot, and so silly, about my being so handy about
a house and things like that. But this thing came on me
suddenly. You'll forgive me, I'm sure.'

'You don't want to say a prayer?' asked Donovan.

'No, chum,' he said. 'I don't think it would help. I'm
ready, and you boys want to get it over.'

'You understand that we're only doing our duty?'
said Donovan.

Belcher's head was raised like a blind man's, so that
you could only see his chin and the top of his nose in
the lantern-light.

'I never could make out what duty was myself,' he
said. 'I think you're all good lads, if that's what you mean.
I'm not complaining.'

Noble, just as if he couldn't bear any more of it, raised
his fist at Donovan, and in a flash Donovan raised his
gun and fired. The big man went over like a sack of
meal, and this time there was no need of a second shot.

I don't remember much about the burying, but that it
was worse than all the rest because we had to carry them
to the grave. It was all mad lonely with nothing but a
patch of lantern-light between ourselves and the dark,
and birds hooting and screeching all round, disturbed

by the guns. Noble went through Hawkins's belongings to find the letter from his mother, and then joined his hands together. He did the same with Belcher. Then, when we'd filled in the grave, we separated from Jeremiah Donovan and Feeney and took our tools back to the shed. All the way we didn't speak a word. The kitchen was dark and cold as we'd left it, and the old woman was sitting over the hearth, saying her beads. We walked past her into the room, and Noble struck a match to light the lamp. She rose quietly and came to the doorway with all her cantankerousness gone.

'What did ye do with them?' she asked in a whisper, and Noble started so that the match went out in his hand.

'What's that?' he asked without turning round.

'I heard ye,' she said.

'What did you hear?' asked Noble.

'I heard ye. Do ye think I didn't hear ye, putting the spade back in the houseen?'

Noble struck another match and this time the lamp lit for him.

'Was that what ye did to them?' she asked.

Then, by God, in the very doorway, she fell on her knees and began praying, and after looking at her for a minute or two Noble did the same by the fireplace. I pushed my way out past her and left them at it. I stood at the door, watching the stars and listening to the shrieking of the birds dying out over the bogs. It is so strange what you feel at times like that that you can't describe it. Noble says he saw everything ten times the size, as though there were nothing in the whole world but that little patch of bog with the two Englishmen stiffening into it, but with me it was as if the patch of bog where the Englishmen were was a million miles away, and even Noble and the old woman, mumbling behind me, and the birds and the bloody stars were all far away, and I was somehow very small and very lost and lonely like a child astray in the snow. And anything that happened to me afterwards, I never felt the same about again.

A Story by Maupassant

People who have not grown up in a provincial town won't know what I mean when I say what Terry Coughlan meant to me. People who have won't need to know.

As kids we lived a few doors from each other on the same terrace, and his sister, Tess, was a friend of my sister, Nan. There was a time when I was rather keen on Tess myself. She was a small, plump, gay little thing, with rosy cheeks like apples, and she played the piano very well. In those days I sang a bit, though I hadn't much of a voice. When I sang Mozart, Beethoven, or even Wagner, Terry would listen with brooding approval. When I sang commonplace stuff, Terry would make a face and walk out. He was a good-looking lad with a big brow and curly black hair, a long, pale face and a pair of intent dark eyes. He was always well spoken and smart in his appearance. There was nothing sloppy about him.

When he could not learn something by night he got up at five in the morning to do it, and whatever he took up, he mastered. Even as a boy he was always looking forward to the day when he'd have money enough to travel, and he taught himself French and German in the time it took me to find out I could not learn Irish. He was cross with me for wanting to learn it; according to him it had 'no cultural significance', but he was crosser still with me because I couldn't learn it. 'The first thing you should learn to do is to work,' he would say gloomily. 'What's going to become of you if you don't?' He had read somewhere that when Keats was depressed, he had a wash and brush up. Keats was his god. Poetry was never much in my line, except Shelley, and Terry didn't think much of him.

We argued about it on our evening walks. Maybe you don't remember the sort of arguments you had when you were young. Lots of people prefer not to remember, but I like thinking of them. A man is never more himself than when he talks nonsense about God, Eternity, prostitution, and the necessity for having mistresses. I argued with Terry that the day of poetry was over, and that the big boys of modern literature were the fiction writers – the ones we'd heard of in Cork at that time, I mean – the Russians and Maupassant.

'The Russians are all right,' he said to me once. 'Maupassant you can forget.'

'But why, Terry?' I asked.

'Because whatever you say about the Russians, they're noble,' he said. 'Noble' was a great word of his at the time: Shakespeare was 'noble', Turgenev was 'noble', Beethoven was 'noble'. 'They are a religious people, like the Greeks, or the English of Shakespeare's time. But Maupassant is slick and coarse and commonplace. Are his stories literature?'

'Ah, to hell with literature!' I said. 'It's life.'

'Life in this country?'

'Life in his own country, then.'

'But how do you know?' Terry asked, stopping and staring at me. 'Humanity is the same here as anywhere else. If he's not true of the life we know, he's not true of any sort of life.'

Then he got the job in the monks' school and I got the job in Carmody's and we began to drift apart. There was no quarrel. It was just that I liked company and Terry didn't. I got in with a wild group – Marshall and Redmond and Donnelan, the solicitor – and we sat up until morning, drinking and settling the future of humanity. Terry came with us once, but he didn't talk, and when Donnelan began to hold forth on Shaw and the Life Force I could see his face getting dark. You know Donnelan's line – 'But what I mean – what I want to say – Jasus, will somebody let me talk? I have something important to say.' We all knew that Donnelan was a bit of a joke, but when I said good-night to Terry in the hall he turned on me with an angry look.

'Do those friends of yours do anything but talk?' he asked.

'Never mind, Terry,' I said. 'The Revolution is coming.'

'Not if they have anything to say to it,' Terry said, and walked away from me. I stood there for a while, feeling sorry for myself, as you do when you know that the end of a friendship is in sight. It didn't make me happier when I went back to the room and Donnelan looked at me as if he didn't believe his eyes.

'Magner,' he asked, 'am I dreaming or was there someone with you?'

Suddenly, for no particular reason, I lost my temper.

'Yes, Donnelan,' I said. 'But somebody I wouldn't expect you to recognize.'

That, I suppose, was the last flash of the old love, and after that it was bogged down in argument. Donnelan said that Terry lacked flexibility – flexibility!

Occasionally I met Tess with her little shopping basket and her round rosy cheeks, and she would say reproachfully, 'Ah, Ted, aren't you becoming a great stranger? What did we do to you at all?' And a couple of times I dropped round to sing a song and borrow a book, and Terry told me about his work as a teacher. He was a bit disillusioned with his job, and you wouldn't wonder.

Some of the monks kept a mackintosh and muffler handy so that they could drop out to the pictures after dark with some doll. And then there was a thundering row when Terry discovered that a couple of his brightest boys were being sent up for public examinations under the names of notorious ignoramuses, so as to bolster up the record. When Brother Dunphy, the headmaster, argued with Terry that it was only a simple act of charity, Terry replied sourly that it seemed to him more like a criminal offence. After that he got the reputation of being impossible and was not consulted when Patrick Dempsey, the boy he really liked, was put up for examination as Mike MacNamara, the County Councillor's son – Mike the Moke, as Terry called him.

Now, Donnelan is a gas-bag, and, speaking charitably, a bit of a fool, but there were certain things he learned in his Barrack Street slum. One night he said to me, 'Ted, does that fellow Coughlan drink?' 'Drink?' I said, laughing outright at him. 'Himself and a sparrow would have about the same consumption of liquor.' Nothing ever embarrassed Donnelan, who had the hide of a rhinoceros.

'Well, you might be right,' he said reasonably, 'but, begor, I never saw a sparrow that couldn't hold it.'

I thought myself that Donnelan was dreaming, but next time I met Tess I sounded her. 'How's that brother of yours keeping?' I asked. 'Ah, fine, Ted, why?' she asked, as though she was really surprised. 'Oh, nothing,' I said. 'Somebody was telling me that he wasn't looking well.'

'Ah, he's that way this long time, Ted,' she replied, 'and 'tis nothing only the want of sleep. He studies too hard at night, and then he goes wandering all over the country, trying to work off the excitement. Sure, I'm always at him!'

That satisfied me. I knew Tess couldn't tell me a lie. But then, one moonlight night about six months later, three or four of us were standing outside the hotel – the night porter had kicked us out in the middle of an argument, and we were finishing it there. Two was striking from Shandon when I saw Terry coming up the pavement towards us. I never knew whether he recognized me or not, but all at once he crossed the street, and even I could see that the man was drunk.

'Tell me,' said Donnelan, peering across at him, 'is that a sparrow I see at this hour of night?' All at once he spun round on his heels, splitting his sides with laughing. 'Magner's sparrow!' he said. 'Magner's sparrow!' I hope in comparing Donnelan with a rhinoceros I haven't done injustice to either party.

I saw then what was happening. Terry was drinking all right, but he was drinking unknown to his mother and sister. You might almost say he was drinking unknown to himself. Other people could be drunkards, but not he. So he sat at home reading, or pretending to read, until late at night, and then slunk off to some low pub on the quays where he hoped people wouldn't recognize him, and came home only when he knew his family was in bed.

For a long time I debated with myself about whether I shouldn't talk to him. If I made up my mind to do it once, I did it twenty times. But when I ran into him in town, striding slowly along, and saw the dark, handsome face with the slightly ironic smile, I lost courage. His mind was as keen as ever – it may even have been a shade too keen. He was becoming slightly irritable and arrogant. The manners were as careful and the voice was as pleasant as ever – a little too much so. The way he raised his hat high in the air to some woman who passed and whipped the big handkerchief from his breast pocket reminded me of an old actor going down in the world. The farther down he went the worse the acting got. He wouldn't join me for a drink; no, he had this job that simply must be finished tonight. How could I say to him, 'Terry, for God's sake, give up trying to pretend you have work to do. I know you're an impostor and you're drinking yourself to death.' You couldn't talk like that to a man of his kind. People like him are all of a piece; they have to stand or fall by something inside themselves.

He was forty when his mother died, and by that time it looked as though he'd have Tess on his hands for life as well. I went back to the house with him after the funeral. He was cruelly broken up. I discovered that he had spent his first few weeks abroad that summer and he was full of it. He had stayed in Paris and visited the cathedrals round, and they had made a deep impression on him. He had never seen real architecture before. I had a vague hope that it might have jolted him out of the rut he had been getting into, but I was wrong. It was worse he was getting.

Then, a couple of years later, I was at home one evening, finishing up some work, when a knock came to the door. I opened it myself and saw old Pa Hourigan, the policeman, outside. Pa had a schoolgirl complexion and a white moustache, China-blue eyes and a sour elderly mouth, like a baby who has learned the facts of life too soon. It surprised me because we never did more than pass the time of day.

'May I speak to you for a moment, Mr Magner?' he asked modestly. ''Tis on a rather private matter.'

'You can to be sure, Sergeant,' I said, joking him. 'I'm not a bit afraid. 'Tis years since I played ball on the public street. Have a drink.'

'I never touch it, going on night duty,' he said, coming into the front room. 'I hope you will pardon my calling, but you know I am not a man to interfere in anyone else's private affairs.'

By this time he had me puzzled and a bit anxious. I knew him for an exceptionally retiring man, and he was clearly upset.

'Ah, of course you're not,' I said. 'No one would accuse you of it. Sit down and tell me what the trouble is.'

'Aren't you a friend of Mr Coughlan, the teacher?' he asked.

'I am,' I said.

'Mr Magner,' he said, exploding on me, 'can you do nothing with the man?'

I looked at him for a moment and had a premonition of disaster.

'Is it as bad as that?' I asked.

'It cannot go on, Mr Magner,' he said, shaking his head. 'It cannot go on. I saved him before. Not because he was anything to me, because I hardly knew the man. Not even because of his poor decent sister, though I pity her with my whole heart and soul. It was for the respect I have for education. And you know that, Mr Magner,' he added earnestly, meaning (which was true enough) that I owed it to him that I had never paid a fine for drinking during prohibited hours.

'We all know it, Sergeant,' I said. 'And I assure you, we appreciate it.'

'No one knows, Mr Magner,' he went on, 'what sacrifices Mrs Hourigan and myself made to put that boy of ours through college, and I would not give it to say to him that an educated man could sink so low. But there are others at the barracks who don't think the way I do. I name no names, Mr Magner, but there are those who would be glad to see an educated man humiliated.'

'What is it, Sergeant?' I asked. 'Drink?'

'Mr Magner,' he said indignantly, 'when did I ever interfere with an educated man for drinking? I know when a man has a lot on his mind he cannot always do without stimulants.'

'You don't mean drugs?' I asked. The idea had crossed my mind once or twice.

'No, Mr Magner, I do not,' he said, quivering with indignation. 'I mean those low, loose, abandoned women that I would have whipped and transported.'

If he had told me that Terry had turned into a common thief, I couldn't have been more astonished and horrified. Horrified is the word.

'You don't mind my saying that I find that very hard to believe, Sergeant?' I asked.

'Mr Magner,' he said with great dignity, 'in my calling a man does not use words lightly.'

'I know Terry Coughlan since we were boys together,

and I never as much as heard an unseemly word from him,' I said.

'Then all I can say, Mr Magner, is that I'm glad, very glad that you've never seen him as I have, in a condition I would not compare to the beasts.' There were real tears in the old man's eyes. 'I spoke to him myself about it. At four o'clock this morning I separated him from two of those vile creatures that I knew well were robbing him. I pleaded with him as if he was my own brother. "Mr Coughlan," I said, "what will your soul do at the Judgement?" And Mr Magner, in decent society I would not repeat the disgusting reply he made me.'

'*Corruptio optimi pessima*,' I said to myself.

'That is Latin, Mr Magner,' the old policeman said with real pleasure.

'And it means "Lilies that fester smell far worse than weeds," Sergeant,' I said. 'I don't know if I can do anything. I suppose I'll have to try. If he goes on like this he'll destroy himself, body and soul.'

'Do what you can for his soul, Mr Magner,' whispered the old man, making for the door. 'As for his body, I wouldn't like to answer.' At the door he turned with a mad stare in his blue eyes. 'I would not like to answer,' he repeated, shaking his grey pate again.

It gave me a nasty turn. Pa Hourigan was happy. He

had done his duty but mine still remained to be done. I sat for an hour, thinking about it, and the more I thought, the more hopeless it seemed. Then I put on my hat and went out.

Terry lived at that time in a nice little house on College Road; a little red-brick villa with a bow window. He answered the door himself, a slow, brooding, black-haired man with a long pale face. He didn't let on to be either surprised or pleased.

'Come in,' he said with a crooked smile. 'You're a great stranger, aren't you?'

'You're a bit of a stranger yourself, Terry,' I said jokingly. Then Tess came out, drying her hands in her apron. Her little cheeks were as rosy as ever, but the gloss was gone. I had the feeling that now there was nothing much she didn't know about her brother. Even the nervous smile suggested that she knew what I had come for – of course, old Hourigan must have brought him home.

'Ah, Ted, 'tis a cure for sore eyes to see you,' she said. 'You'll have a cup? You will, to be sure.'

'You'll have a drink,' Terry said.

'Do you know, I think I will, Terry,' I said, seeing a nice natural opening for the sort of talk I had in mind.

'Ah, you may as well have both,' said Tess, and a few minutes later she brought in the tea and cake. It was like old times until she left us, and then it wasn't. Terry poured out the whiskey for me and the tea for himself, though his hand was shaking so badly that he could scarcely lift his cup. It was not all pretence; he didn't want to give me an opening, that was all. There was a fine print over his head – I think it was a Constable of Salisbury Cathedral. He talked about the monastery school, the usual clever, bitter, contemptuous stuff about monks, inspectors, and pupils. The whole thing was too carefully staged, the lifting of the cup and the wiping of the moustache, but it hypnotized me. There was something there you couldn't do violence to. I finished my drink and got up to go.

'What hurry is on you?' he asked irritably.

I mumbled something about it's getting late.

'Nonsense!' he said. 'You're not a boy any longer.'

Was he just showing off his strength of will or hoping to put off the evil hour when he would go slinking down the quays again?

'Ah, they'll be expecting me,' I said, and then, as I used to do when we were younger, I turned to the bookcase. 'I see you have a lot of Maupassant at last,' I said.

'I bought them last time I was in Paris,' he said, standing beside me and looking at the books as though he were seeing them for the first time.

'A death-bed repentance?' I asked lightly, but he ignored me.

'I met another great admirer of his there,' he said sourly. 'A lady you should meet some time.'

'I'd love to if I ever get there,' I said.

'Her address is the Rue de Grenelle,' he said, and then with a wild burst of mockery, 'the left-hand pavement.'

At last his guard was down, and it was Maupassant's name that had done it. And still I couldn't say anything. An angry flush mounted his pale dark face and made it sinister in its violence.

'I suppose you didn't know I indulged in that hideous vice?' he snarled.

'I heard something,' I said. 'I'm sorry, Terry.'

The angry flush died out of his face and the old brooding look came back.

'A funny thing about those books,' he said. 'This woman I was speaking about, I thought she was bringing me to a hotel. I suppose I was a bit muddled with drink, but after dark one of these places is much like another. "This isn't a hotel," I said when we got upstairs. "No," she said, "It's my room."'

As he told it, I could see that he was living it all over again, something he could tell nobody but myself.

'There was a screen in the corner. I suppose it's the result of reading too much romantic fiction, but I thought there might be somebody hidden behind it. There was. You'd never guess what?'

'No.'

'A baby,' he said, his eyes boring through me. 'A child of maybe eighteen months. I wouldn't know. While I was looking, she changed him. He didn't wake.'

'What was it?' I asked, searching for the message that he obviously thought the incident contained. 'A dodge?'

'No,' he said almost grudgingly. 'A country girl in trouble, trying to support her child, that's all. We went to bed and she fell asleep. I couldn't. It's many years now since I've been able to sleep like that. So I put on the light and began to read one of the books that I carried round in my pocket. The light woke her and she wanted to see what I had. "Oh, Maupassant," she said. "He's a great writer." "Is he?" I said. I thought she might be repeating something she'd picked up from one of her customers. She wasn't. She began to talk about *Boule de Suif*. It reminded me of the arguments we used to have in our young days.' Suddenly he gave me a curious boyish smile. 'You remember, when we used to walk up the river together.'

'Oh, I remember,' I said with a sigh.

'We were terrible young idiots, the pair of us,' he said sadly. 'Then she began to talk about *The Tellier Household*.

I said it had poetry. "Oh, if it's poetry you want, you don't go to Maupassant. You go to Vigny, you go to Musset, but Maupassant is life, and life isn't poetry. It's only when you see what life can do to you that you realize what a great writer Maupassant is." . . . Wasn't that an extraordinary thing to happen?' he asked fiercely, and again the angry colour mounted his cheeks.

'Extraordinary,' I said, wondering if Terry himself knew how extraordinary it was. But it was exactly as if he were reading the thoughts as they crossed my mind.

'A prostitute from some French village, a drunken old waster from an Irish provincial town, lying awake in the dawn in Paris, discussing Maupassant. And the baby, of course. Maupassant would have made a lot of the baby.'

'I declare to God, I think if I'd been in your shoes, I'd have brought them back with me,' I said. I knew when I said it that I was talking nonsense, but it was a sort of release for all the bitterness inside me.

'What?' he asked, mocking me. 'A prostitute and her baby? My dear Mr Magner, you're becoming positively romantic in your old age.'

'A man like you should have a wife and children,' I said.

'Ah, but that's a different story,' he said malevolently. 'Maupassant would never have ended a story like that.'

And he looked at me almost triumphantly with those mad, dark eyes. I knew how Maupassant would have ended that story all right. Maupassant, as the girl said, was life, and life was pretty nearly through with Terry Coughlan.

a little history

Penguin Modern Classics were launched in 1961, and have been shaping the reading habits of generations ever since.

The list began with distinctive grey spines and evocative pictorial covers – a look that, after various incarnations, continues to influence their current design – and with books that are still considered landmark classics today.

Penguin Modern Classics have caused scandal and political change, inspired great films and broken down barriers, whether social, sexual or the boundaries of language itself. They remain the most provocative, groundbreaking, exciting and revolutionary works of the last 100 years (or so).

In 2011, on the fiftieth anniversary of the Modern Classics, we're publishing fifty Mini Modern Classics: the very best short fiction by writers ranging from Beckett to Conrad, Nabokov to Saki, Updike to Wodehouse. Though they don't take long to read, they'll stay with you long after you turn the final page.

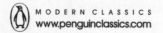

MODERN CLASSICS
www.penguinclassics.com